The Lion and the Mouse

Retold by Susanna Davidson

Illustrated by John Joven

Reading consultant: Alison Kelly

The sun beat down on the dry ground.

"It's much too hot for me," said Chief Mouse. "Let's go back home to our burrow."

"I think I'll stay here," said Little Mouse, "and eat some more seeds."

"You can't stay on your own," said Chief Mouse. "You're too little."

"Follow me everyone,"
said Chief Mouse.

He led them through
clumps of grass...

He led them across
shallow streams...

...and under shady trees.

Poor Little
Mouse couldn't
keep up.

Now he was all alone.

Oh dear!

He was also... LOST!

Ahead, Little Mouse saw a large hill. "I'll climb the hill," he thought.

Then I might be able to see the others.

Little Mouse began
to climb.

"This is a very strange hill," thought Little Mouse.

"It keeps moving up and down."

"I'm beginning to
think it's not a hill
at all..."

Then Little Mouse
turned around.

Little Mouse squeaked so loudly, Lion woke up.

Lion did *not* look happy.

Little Mouse tried to run...

...but Lion caught
   him by the tail.

"You woke me up," said
Lion. "And now I'm going
to EAT YOU!"

22

How Lion laughed!

Ha! Ha! Ha!

26

"As if YOU could ever save ME," he chuckled.

Haaaaaaa!

"But you've made me laugh, little friend, so I'll let you go."

27

Then Little Mouse turned around... and fled.

Little Mouse finally found his burrow. He told the other mice his story.

They all laughed too.

You're the smallest of us all!

As if YOU could ever help a lion!

"Humph," said Little
Mouse. "Just you wait
and see."

They didn't have to
wait long...

That very night, Lion
walked straight into
a hunter's trap.

He thrashed and roared
and tried to claw his
way out.

The net held tight.

In his snug burrow, Little Mouse heard Lion's roars.

Roarrrrrrrrr!

"Lion is in trouble!" said Little Mouse. "I must go to him."

"You won't be able to help him," said Chief Mouse. "You're TOO SMALL."

"But I made a promise," said Little Mouse.

"And mice keep their promises."

Little Mouse went
out into the night.

He followed the sound of
the roars.

37

At last, he found Lion
in a huge net.

"Have you come to laugh
at me?" snarled Lion.

All night, Little Mouse
nibbled and gnawed at
the ropes.

At first light,
the net broke.

"You saved my life,"
said Lion.

"I see that little friends
can be great friends,
after all."

Little Mouse puffed himself up with pride.

"Is there anything I can do for *you*, Little Mouse?" asked Lion.

"Actually," said Little Mouse. "There is *one* thing..."

About the story

Aesop's Fables are from Ancient Greece.
They always have a moral, or a lesson, at
the end. The moral of this story is:
"The small can help the strong."

Designed by Vickie Robinson
Series designer: Russell Punter
Series editor: Lesley Sims

First published in 2019 by Usborne Publishing Ltd.,
Usborne House, 83-85 Saffron Hill, London EC1N 8RT, England.
www.usborne.com Copyright © 2019 Usborne Publishing Ltd.